In loving memory of my Grandparents

Melanie
Kassen

Acknowledgments

A multitude of gratitude to James B. Gajunera, Illustrator. Without his originality, Bruce, Juliet, and all these wonderful critters and images would never have made it into our hearts! I am forever humbled by your talent!

Much appreciation to The Synthesizer. It all started with two plushy toys. Great job on finding James! The project would have stagnated without your persistence screening all the applicants and insistence that the project move forward. Thank you, also, for making the transitions smoother and putting those necessary finishing touches to the text.

ISBN: 1489559515
ISBN 13: 9781489559517
Library of Congress Control Number: 2013910077
CreateSpace Independent Publishing Platform
North Charleston, South Carolina

Thank you to Bruce and Juliet for trusting me with their story. They certainly were excited to tell it!

Thank you to my younger sister, Marina, for reading the first draft and liking it!

Thank you, also, to all my teachers who encouraged and challenged me.

Much gratitude to my friends who supported my efforts regardless...you know who you are.

To everyone on "CreateSpace Team 2": Jack, Lynn, Jesse, Andrea Liz, Nicole, Chelsea, Erin and counting...

Thank you for this journey!

ONCE UPON A TIME, deep in a lush, green forest, there was a wondrous cave. Inside this cave lived a father dragon, a mother dragon, and their young dragon son, Bruce. Dracco, the father, came from a long line of fire-breathing dragons. His father, his father's father, and his father's father's father all breathed fire! Dracco's wife, Mala, loved both her husband and her son dearly.

Bruce grew up quickly. His wings filled out nicely, his legs grew stronger, and his confidence soared with all the loving support from his wonderful family. Bruce's father anxiously waited for the day when he'd teach his young son the family business of being a fierce, fire-breathing dragon.

When that big day arrived, his parents began training Bruce in a vast clearing in the forest. Dracco set up targets and breathed fire to demonstrate his expertise. Hitting target after target with perfect accuracy, Dracco showcased all of his incredible skills for Bruce. He even hit his final target, a large, old tree stump, while standing on one foot, with one eye closed! Astonished by his father's remarkable talents, Bruce's eyes twinkled with delight and admiration. He recognized that his father was the greatest of all living dragons and he wanted to be just like him.

Eventually it was Bruce's turn to try. He gathered his courage, closed his eyes tightly, concentrated really hard, took a few deep breaths, and blew and blew and blew. Bruce then opened his eyes slowly, noticing very surprised looks on his parents' faces. They were looking toward the sky, and Bruce glanced up to see what his parents were seeing—there were bubbles, bubbles, and still more bubbles!

So Bruce tried again, thinking fire would come out on the second try for sure. He left his eyes open, but there they were again—more bubbles! Wow, how could this be? A bubble-breathing dragon? No one in the family had ever heard of such a thing.

On the way back to the family cave, no one could speak a word. Dracco and Mala had never expected this to happen, not from a member of their long line of fire-breathing dragons. They all felt confused. Upon arriving back home, Bruce retreated to his room. He was upset about what had transpired and thought that he had become quite a disappointment to his parents. He wouldn't even come out for dinner that night.

The next day, after a good night's sleep and a healthy breakfast, Bruce decided that he wanted to have another fire-breathing lesson. Dracco took Bruce back to the clearing for more practice. Nervous and excited, Bruce tried again and again and again to breathe fire. But once again, no luck-just bubbles.

Tired and frustrated after a long day of training, father and son returned home to Mala. Inconsolable, Bruce went to his room. His loving parents tried to comfort him and talk to him, but Bruce just wanted to be left alone. He truly felt like he had failed his family.

That night, while his parents slept, young Bruce decided to leave home and set out on his own. He hoped to find answers to his problem. What could he possibly do in the world if he was a dragon who breathed bubbles instead of fire? All he had ever dreamed of his whole life was being just like his father-a brave fire-breathing dragon.

What was he supposed to do now?

As Bruce ventured out, the night darkened and it soon grew very cold. It seemed he had traveled far from home, outside his beloved forest and all he knew. He heard so many loud night noises-owls hooting, crickets chirping, and even a few mysterious howling sounds.

Bruce was frightened now by the darkness and the strange noises, and he soon realized he would need some shelter for the night. He eventually stumbled upon a hollowed-out tree stump where he felt he would be safe for the night. In his sleep, he dreamed of many splendorous things-magical feats of breathing fire and happy looks of approval on his parents' faces. Contented by his dreams, he awakened in the morning only to feel sad again when he remembered that he was a dragon who was unable to breathe fire.

Just then, he heard an unfamiliar sound coming from not so far away. Cautiously sticking his head out from behind the log, he saw the deep grass of a dewy, sun-kissed meadow. And then he heard a quiet voice approaching him. Remaining very still, Bruce waited to see if it was safe to come out.

Soon enough, the voice got closer to him. It sounded like a girl's voice, and it sounded like she was talking to herself. She seemed frustrated and grumpy. Bruce thought he heard her say something about not being able to catch butterflies. By the tone of her voice, Bruce sensed that it was safe for him to come out.

Immediately, he saw the creature he had heard talking to herself.

She was a kitten!

They noticed one another at the same exact moment and froze in their tracks, each staring at the other. After a few moments of slowly circling one another, they decided it was safe to introduce themselves. Bruce learned that the kitten's name was Juliet. Juliet explained that she liked to daydream a lot and that she had wandered away from her mother into the meadow very early that morning to chase butterflies. Juliet said that her mother was very aware of how much her daughter enjoyed adventure.

Bruce and Juliet started talking more with each other about their favorite things and about their different lives at home. Juliet told Bruce how she liked to chase butterflies but unfortunately she could not catch them very well. She explained to Bruce that they simply moved too fast and she could not keep up with them. She told him she needed to keep practicing to improve her butterfly-catching skills when she wasn't in the meadow daydreaming.

Bruce then confided all of his woes to Juliet. He told her everything-how he came from a long line of fire-breathing dragons and how all he ever wanted in life was to become a fire-breathing dragon, but that no matter how hard he tried, he could only breathe bubbles. Juliet giggled. She had never heard of such a crazy thing! It couldn't possibly be true, could it? Bruce reassured her that it was in fact very true, but he was too embarrassed to give her a demonstration. Juliet begged him to show her. Although he was still feeling somewhat insecure about breathing bubbles, Bruce finally agreed.

Bruce breathed out tons of bubbles. Juliet instantly delighted in this and began chasing them around the meadow with great joy, catching and popping them in the air one by one. She chased so many that she eventually ran out of breath. Running back to Bruce, she begged him for more bubbles. He refused at first, believing that she was only making fun of him. Juliet reassured Bruce that she was not making fun of him at all; in fact just the opposite was true. After catching her breath, Juliet explained how exhilarating it felt to chase and catch Bruce's bubbles.

It wasn't frustrating at all to chase bubbles, she explained, nothing like when she chased butterflies. Again, she asked Bruce for more practice bubbles. She was very confident that if she chased after more bubbles, she would become the best butterfly catcher ever! Bruce obliged. He breathed out another round of bubbles for Juliet. If he couldn't breathe fire, he figured at least he could be happy to help his new friend improve her bubble-catching coordination. And so they continued to play in the meadow for hours.

As the sun began to set, Juliet heard her mother calling for her. She asked Bruce to come with her. She wanted very much to show her mother that for once in her life she hadn't been daydreaming. Bruce thought he should return home instead, but night was already falling and he realized he was very far from home.

So Bruce followed Juliet through the meadow and across the stream to a grand tree house where Juliet lived with her mother, Suzette. When they arrived, her mother was both pleased and shocked. She hugged Juliet but also stared curiously at her dragon friend Bruce. Juliet explained how she had met Bruce accidentally and had spent the whole afternoon chasing bubbles. Suzette graciously welcomed Bruce to sit down with them and share their meal. Even though Bruce appeared very kind, Suzette was still very cautious around him. This was the first time any cat in her family had been in the same room with a dragon of any kind. She certainly never imagined dragons could be so friendly!

After a lively evening swapping stories of dragon life and cat life, Suzette made a place for Bruce to sleep and then tucked in Juliet for the night.

Filled with gratitude for his new friends and also for his warm bed, Bruce realized running away from his family and problems was not just a poor choice for a solution, but he was now certain his parents would be very worried about him. As he fell into a deep slumber, he decided that tomorrow he would return to face his parents and apologize for running away.

After a good night's sleep, they woke up to a beautiful day. Suzette fed Bruce and Juliet a healthy breakfast and they all set out together from the tree house, back across the stream and through the meadow toward the green, lush forest where Bruce's family lived.

Along the way, Bruce breathed bubbles and Juliet chased them, catching and popping them ever more skillfully each time. This impressed Juliet's mother greatly. Suzette worried about Juliet at times, but she could now see that her daughter's unlikely friendship with Bruce, the bubble-breathing dragon, had taught Juliet better coordination and patience-and cut down on her daydreaming!

After a full day's journey back to the forest, Suzette, Juliet, and Bruce finally arrived at Bruce's family cave. Bruce knew he would be in trouble, and he was ready to explain and apologize to his parents. He entered the cave and called out to his parents. They rushed to greet him and hug him. He could then see his mother had been crying. Dracco was about to breathe out a fireball because he was so upset with himself and now he felt regretful for being way too hard on Bruce.

Following the tearful, yet joyful, reunion, Bruce introduced his parents to Juliet and her mother. They were as dumbfounded by this friendship as Suzette had been the day before. Nevertheless, they were all on their best behavior. Mala brought out drinks and snacks, which everyone shared.

Bruce and Juliet asked to be excused so they could practice breathing and chasing bubbles a bit more before dark. As they ran off, Suzette expressed her gratitude to Mala and Dracco for raising such a genuinely kind and thoughtful young dragon. She was eternally grateful Bruce had happened along when he did to help Juliet develop her bubble-catching skills and, more importantly, her confidence. She thought that Juliet's self-esteem seemed to increase overnight.

Bruce's parents could only smile. How amazing was it that through all the frustration, tears, and anxiety everyone could end up relieved and grateful? Bruce may have been unable to breathe fire, but his bubbles taught Juliet the coordination she had needed to chase butterflies more skillfully. In addition, new friendships, perhaps even lifelong friendships, had been made as a result of this miraculous connection.

Bruce and Juliet and their families remained friends all their lives. Harnessing their skills as a bubble breather and a butterfly catcher, Bruce and Juliet decided to start a "Fitness and Fun Camp" for kittens. Juliet recruited kittens from all around and brought them to train at the camp. Bruce was in charge of creating all sorts of clever obstacle courses for the kittens to help them sharpen their bubble-catching skills. This process began with the kittens chasing the bubbles that he breathed, and then they advanced to the next level and chased butterflies and other faster-moving critters throughout the meadow.

Opening the camp filled Bruce and Juliet with great happiness and joy.

Many years soon passed. It was a long time since the days of their innocent youth, a time when they'd once felt they weren't good enough being exactly who they were. But luckily they'd discovered each other at just the right time, each helping the other develop and flourish because of their own unique skills. Working together, combining their mutual strengths, they learned to believe in themselves and helped others believe in themselves, too. Bruce the bubble-breathing dragon and Juliet the daydreaming kitten were able to accomplish much more as a union than they ever would have achieved working alone, thanks to their trust and encouragement and a very unlikely friendship.